DOG ON A LOG™
Pup Books
Book 3

I am not a Reading Specialist or certified educator, but I do have a lot of experience teaching my daughter with dyslexia how to read. At times, it was difficult to determine what to do and how to do it. It is my hope that the information provided within this book will make the journey a bit easier for other parents. The content provided herein is for informational purposes and does not take the place of an evaluation and teaching plan provided by a credentialed educator. Every effort has been made to ensure that the content provided here is accurate and helpful for my readers. However, this is not an exhaustive treatment of the subject. No liability is assumed for losses or damages due to the information provided. You should consult a credentialed educator for specific guidance on educating your child, yourself, or others.

DOG ON A LOG Books
Tucson, Arizona

Public Domain images from www.clker.com

ISBN: 978-1949471915

Library of Congress
Control Number:2019906065

www.dogonalogbooks.com

KIDS' SQUIGGLES
(LETTERS MAKE WORDS)
DOG ON A LOG Pup Books 3

A Kids' Companion to
THE SQUIGGLE CODE
(LETTERS MAKE WORDS)

By Pamela Brookes
Edited by Nancy Mather Ph.D.

For Parents and Teachers,

Scientific research has shown that the best way for most people to learn to read is by using phonics.[1] This book is a beginning phonics reader. Like all DOG ON A LOG Books, it was written with a progression of letters/sounds to help your child learn to read by mastering a small step of letters, sight words, or phonics rules before moving on to the next step of phonics rules.

This is the kids' companion book to *THE SQUIGGLE CODE (LETTERS MAKE WORDS.)* The stories in here are also in *The Squiggle Code.* However, they are in a more child-friendly format in this book. There are only one or two sentences per page and there are pictures for each page of text. If buying both books is out of your budget, check your local library to see if they have them. If you can only buy one book, buy *The Squiggle Code* as it gives guidance and has more materials than this book.

---

[1] *Put Reading First*, Third Edition, Center for the Improvement of Early Reading Achievement (CIERA) and funded by the National Institute for Literacy (NIFL) https://lincs.ed.gov/publications/pdf/PRFbooklet.pdf

The Squiggle Code is a roadmap for teaching your child to read. It gives guidance on how to introduce letters and reading to your child. Before using *The Squiggle Code,* your child should have mastered the skills in *Before the Squiggle Code (A Roadmap to Reading.)*

For more materials and activities, please see the printables available at www.dogonalogbooks.com.

A Note about Pictures.
The pictures are included to break up the reading. Even a four-word sentence can be a lot for a new reader, especially if the child is struggling to learn. However, do not ask your child to guess what the word is based on the picture. That does not teach kids how to sound out and read words, it teaches them to guess. My recommendation would be to cover the picture with a sheet of paper. When the child successfully decodes (sounds out) the sentence, then you can pull away the paper and get the reward of seeing the picture.

Tup says, "Ruff, ruff."

Happy Reading, Pamela Brookes

Download DOG ON A LOG printable gameboards, games, flashcards, and other activities at:
www.dogonalogbooks.com/printables.

Parents and Teachers:
Receive email notifications of new books and printables. Sign up at:
www.dogonalogbooks.com/subscribe

Table of Contents

DOG ON A LOG
Parent and Teacher Guides

General Information
on Dyslexia and
Struggling Readers

The Author's Routine
for Teaching Reading

Book 1. *Teaching a Struggling Reader: One Mom's Experience with Dyslexia*

Book 2. *How to Use Decodable Books to Teach Reading*

Available for free from many online booksellers or read at:
www.dogonalogbooks.com/free

Nan Fam

Letter Group 1
a, s, m, f, t, n

Sight Words
is, the

Nan Fam is tan.

Nan Fam sat.

Tan Nan Fam sat.

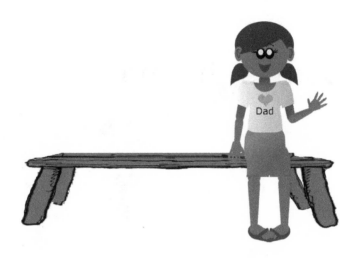

Sam is the man.

The man is Sam Fam.

Sam Fam sat.

Sam Fam the man sat.

Sam Fam is the man.

Tag

Letter Group 2
r, d, c, g

New Sight Words
a, and, to, has

Dan has a cat.

The cat is Tam.

Tam the cat ran to tag Dan.

Dan ran to tag Tad.

Tad is a ram.

Tad the ram ran to tag Dad.

Dad ran.

Dan ran to tag Tam
the cat.

Tam the cat ran and ran.

The Tot

Letter Group 3
o

Don is a tot.

Don sat on a cat.

Don sat on a cod.

The cat got mad.

The cod got mad.

Don is sad.

Don got the cat a mat.

Don got the cod a cot.

The cat is not mad.

The cod is not mad.

Don is not sad.

Max and Sal

Letter Group 4
b, h, l, x

New Sight Words
does, go, of

Max and Sal ran to the cab.

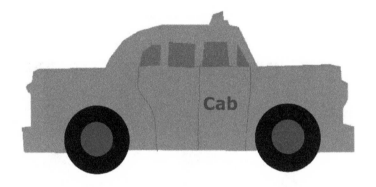

The cab has a lot of gas.

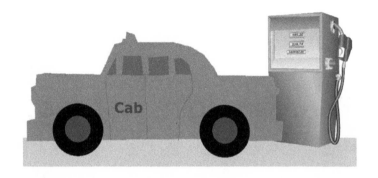

The cab does not lag.

The cab can go and go and go.

The cab got to the bog.

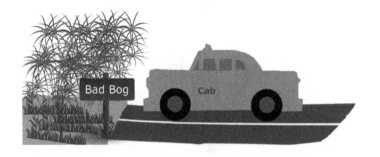

Bad Bog

Cab

The bog is hot.

Bad Bog

Cab

The cab does go to the dam.

Max and Sal got to the dam.

The dam is not hot.

Max and Sal gab and gab and gab at the dam.

Bip, Sop, Lob

Letter Group 5
i, p, k, j

New Sight Words
her, says

Jan has a lid.

Jan does tap the lid.

The lid says, "Bip, bop, dop."

Jan has a sis.

Her sis has a pan.

Sis does tap the pan.

The pan says, "Sop, sop, sop."

Mom has a mop.

Mom does tap the mop on the mat.

The mop says, "Lip, dop, lop."

Dad does sit on the mat.

Dad does nod to the tap, tap, tap.

Dad does nod to the, "Bip, sop, lop."

Jan and Quin

Letter Group 6
u, y, z, qu

Jan has a pal.

Her pal is Quin.

Quin has a pup. The pup is his pal.

The pup says, "Yap, yap."

Jan has a dog. Her dog is Tup.

Tup says, "Yip, yip."

Jan says to Quin, "Let us go for a run."

Jan and Tup run zig.

Quin and his pup run zag.

Jan and Quin zig and zag and run, run, run.

Wet Van

Letter Group 7
e, v, w

Jan and Quin are wet.

Jan and her dad are wet.

Dad and the van are wet.

Jan has a rag. A wet rag.

Jan does rub the wet rag on the van.

Quin has mop. A wet mop.

Quin does rub the wet mop on the van.

Dad has a wet rag.

Dad does rub the top of the van.

Dad has a rag. It is not wet.

He does rub the van.

The van is not wet.

Sight Words used in "Kids' Squiggles"

Letter Group 1: the, is

Letter Group 2: a, and, to, has

Letter Group 4: does, go, of

Letter Group 5: her, says

KEYWORDS

Alphabet

Aa	Bb
apple	bat
Cc	Dd
cat	dog

Ee  _Ed	Ff _fun
Gg _game	Hh _hat
Ii _itch	Jj _jug

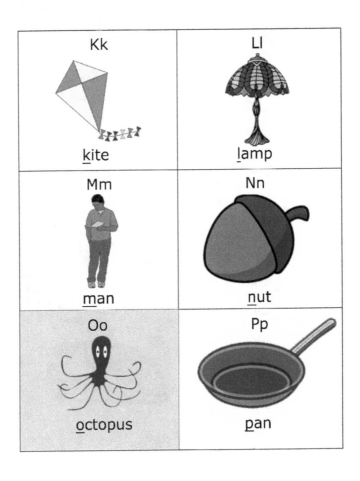

Kk	Ll
kite	lamp
Mm	Nn
man	nut
Oo	Pp
octopus	pan

Qu qu	Rr
<u>qu</u>een	<u>r</u>at
Ss	Tt
<u>s</u>nake	<u>t</u>op
Uu	Vv
<u>u</u>p	<u>v</u>an

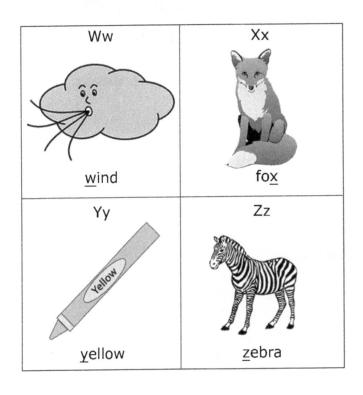

Ww	Xx
wind	fox
Yy	Zz
yellow	zebra

DOG ON A LOG Books
Phonics Progression

DOG ON A LOG Pup Books
Book 1
Phonological/Phonemic Awareness:
- Words
- Rhyming
- Syllables, identification, blending, segmenting
- Identifying individual letter sounds

Books 2-3
Phonemic Awareness/Phonics
- Consonants, primary sounds
- Short vowels
- Blending
- Introduction to sight words

DOG ON A LOG Let's GO! and Chapter Books

Step 1
- Consonants, primary sounds
- Short vowels
- Digraphs: ch, sh, th, wh, ck
- 2 and 3 sound words
- Possessive 's

Step 2
- Bonus letters (f, l, s, z after short vowel)
- "all"
- –s suffix

Step 3
- Letter Buddies: ang, ing, ong, ung, ank, ink, onk, unk

Step 4
- Consonant blends to make 4 sound words
- 3 and 4 sound words ending in –lk, -sk

Step 5
- Digraph blend –nch to make 3 and 4 sound words
- Silent e, including "-ke"

Step 6
- Exception words containing: ild, old, olt, ind, ost

Step 7
- 5 sounds in a closed syllable word plus suffix -s (crunch, slumps)
- 3 letter blends and up to 6 sounds in a closed syllable word (script, spring)

Step 8

- Two syllable words with 2 closed syllables, not blends (sunset, chicken, unlock)

Step 9

- Two syllable words with all previously introduced sounds including blends, exception words, and silent "e" (blacksmith, kindness, inside)
- Vowel digraphs: ai, ay, ea, ee, ie, oa, oe (rain, play, beach, tree, pie, goat, toe)

Let's GO! Books have less text

Chapter Books are longer

WATCH FOR MORE STEPS COMING SOON

DOG ON A LOG Books
Sight Word Progression

DOG ON A LOG Pup Books
a, does, go, has, her is, of, says, the, to

DOG ON A LOG Let's GO! and Chapter Books

Step 1
a, are, be, does, go, goes, has, he, her, his, into, is, like, my, of, OK, says, see, she, the, they, to, want, you

Step 2
could, do, eggs, for, from, have, here, I, likes, me, nest, onto, or, puts, said, say, sees, should, wants, was, we, what, would, your

Step 3
as, Mr., Mrs., no, put, their, there, where

Step 4
push, saw

Step 5
come, comes, egg, pull, pulls, talk, walk, walks

Step 6
Ms., so, some, talks

Step 7
Hmmm, our, out, Pop E., TV

Step 8
Dr., friend, full, hi, island, people, please

More DOG ON A LOG Books

Most books available in Paperback, Hardback, and e-book formats

DOG ON A LOG Parent and Teacher Guides

Book 1 (Also in FREE e-book and PDF Bookfold)
- Teaching a Struggling Reader: One Mom's Experience with Dyslexia

Book 2 (FREE e-book and PDF Bookfold only)
- How to Use Decodable Books to Teach Reading

DOG ON A LOG Pup Books
Book 1
- Before the Squiggle Code (A Roadmap to Reading)

Books 2-3
- The Squiggle Code (Letters Make Words)
- Kids' Squiggles (Letters Make Words)

DOG ON A LOG Let's GO! and Chapter Books

Step 1
- The Dog on the Log
- The Pig Hat
- Chad the Cat
- Zip the Bug
- The Fish and the Pig

Step 2
- Mud on the Path
- The Red Hen
- The Hat and Bug Shop
- Babs the 'Bot
- The Cub

Step 3
- Mr. Bing has Hen Dots
- The Junk Lot Cat
- Bonk Punk Hot Rod
- The Ship with Wings
- The Sub in the Fish Tank

Step 4
- The Push Truck
- The Sand Hill
- Lil Tilt and Mr. Ling
- Musk Ox in the Tub
- The Trip to the Pond

Step 5
- Bake a Cake
- The Crane at the Cave
- Ride a Bike
- Crane or Crane?
- The Swing Gate

Step 6

- The Colt
- The Gold Bolt
- Hide in the Blinds
- The Stone Child
- Tolt the Kind Cat

Step 7

- Quest for A Grump Grunt
- The Blimp
- The Spring in the Lane
- Stamp for a Note
- Stripes and Splats

Step 8

- Anvil and Magnet
- The Mascot
- Kevin's Rabbit Hole
- The Humbug Vet and Medic Shop
- Chickens in the Attic

Step 9

- Trip to Cactus Gulch 1: The Step-Up Team
- Trip to Cactus Gulch 2: Into the Mineshaft
- Play the Bagpipes
- The Hidden Tale 1: The Lost Snapshot

All chapter books can be purchased individually or with all the same-step books in one volume.

Steps 1-5 can be bought as Let's GO! Books which are less text companions to the chapter books.

All titles can be bought as chapter books.

WATCH FOR MORE BOOKS COMING SOON

How You Can Help

Parents often worry that their child (or even adult learner) is not going to learn to read. Hearing other people's successes (especially when they struggled) can give worried parents or teachers hope. I would encourage others to share their experiences with products you've used by posting reviews at your favorite bookseller(s) stating how your child benefitted from those books or materials (whether it was DOG ON A LOG Books or another book or product.) This will help other parents and teachers know which products they should consider using. More than that, hearing your successes could truly help another family feel hopeful. It's amazing that something as seemingly small as a review can ease someone's concerns.

DOG ON A LOG Quick Assessment

Have your child read the following words. If they can't read every word in a Step, that is probably where in the series they should start. Get a printable assessment sheet at: www.dogonalogbooks.com/how-to-use/assessment-tool/

Step 1
fin, mash, sock, sub, cat, that, Dan's

Step 2
less, bats, tell, mall, chips, whiff, falls

Step 3
bangs, dank, honk, pings, chunk, sink, gong, rungs

Step 4
silk, fluff, smash, krill, drop, slim, whisk

Step 5
hunch, crate, rake, tote, inch, mote, lime

Step 6
child, molts, fold, hind, jolt, post, colds

Step 7
strive, scrape, splint, twists, crunch, prints, blend

Step 8
finish, denim, within, bathtub, sunset, medic, habit

Step 9
hundred, goldfinch, free, wheat, inhale, play, Joe

CPSIA information can be obtained
at www.ICGtesting.com
Printed in the USA
LVHW111331020622
720240LV00003B/36